MISSIONS OF THE U.S. NAVY SEALs

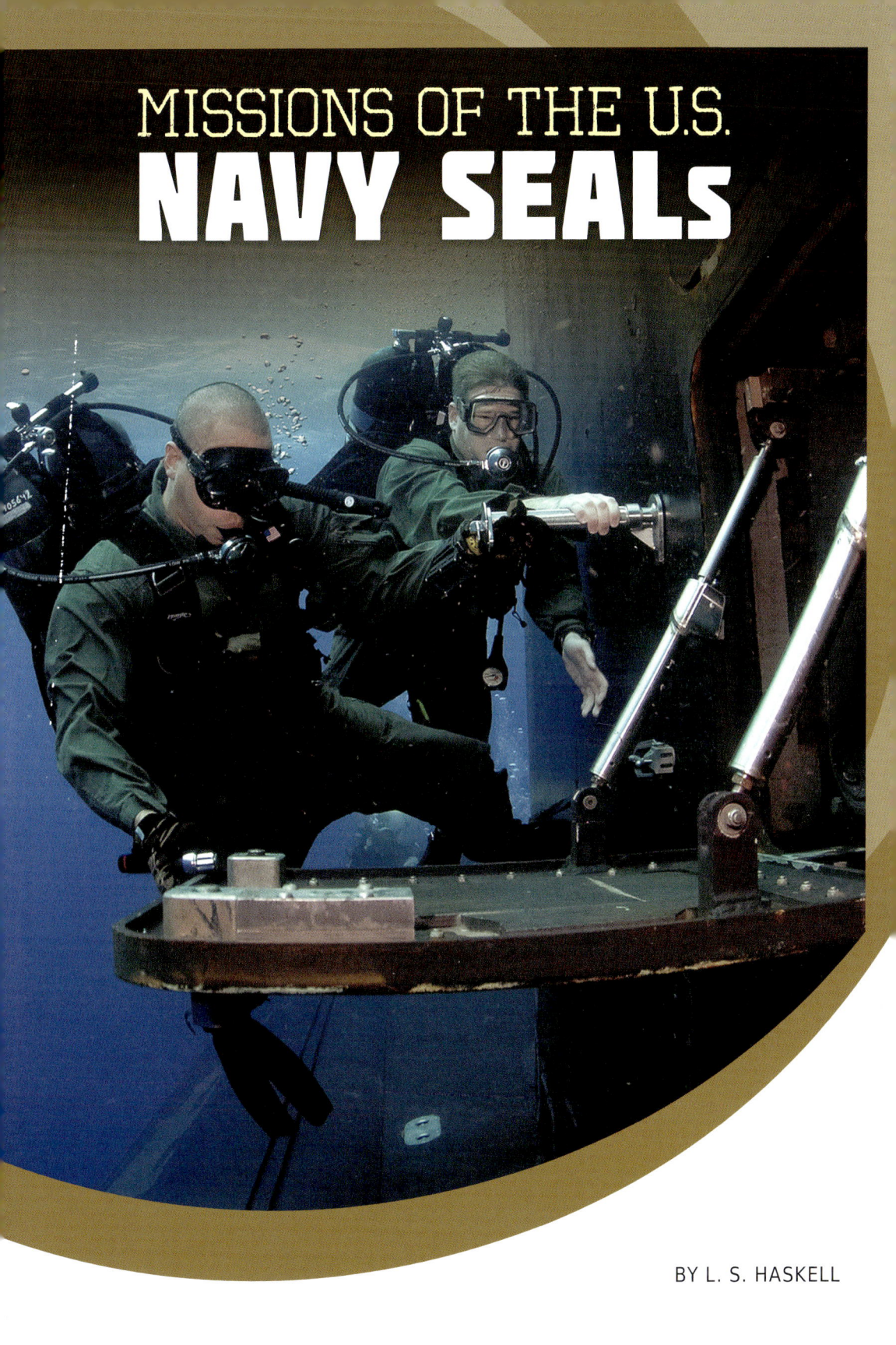

BY L. S. HASKELL

The Child's World®
childsworld.com

Published by The Child's World®
1980 Lookout Drive • Mankato, MN 56003-1705
800-599-READ • www.childsworld.com

Acknowledgments
The Child's World®: Mary Berendes, Publishing Director
Red Line Editorial: Design, editorial direction, and production
Photographs ©: Senior Chief Mass Communication Specialist Andrew McKaskle/U.S. Navy, cover, 1; Mass Communication Specialist Gregory A. Harden II/U.S. Navy, 5; Petty Officer 3rd Class Blake R. Midnight/U.S. Navy/U.S. Department of Defense, 6; Lt. Frederick Martin/U.S. Navy, 8; Cherie Cullen/U.S. Department of Defense, 9; Bettmann/Corbis, 10; PH1 R. Oriez/U.S. Department of Defense, 12; Petty Officer 2nd Class Meranda Keller/U.S. Navy, 14; Spc. David Marck Jr./U.S. Army, 16, 17; Photographer's Mate 2nd Class Andrew M. Meyers/U.S. Navy, 18; Petty Officer 3rd Class Adam Henderson/U.S. Navy, 20; Journalist 2nd Class Wes Eplen/U.S. Navy, 21

Copyright © 2016 by The Child's World®
All rights reserved. No part of this book may be reproduced or utilized in any form or by any means without written permission from the publisher.

ISBN 9781634074469

LCCN 2015946293

Printed in the United States of America
Mankato, MN
December, 2015
PA02285

TABLE OF CONTENTS

ABOUT THE U.S. NAVY SEALs 4

Chapter 1
THE ONLY EASY DAY WAS YESTERDAY 6

Chapter 2
LEAVE NO MAN BEHIND 10

Chapter 3
NEVER GIVE UP 12

Chapter 4
FIGHT TO WIN 14

Chapter 5
FAILURE IS NOT AN OPTION 18

Glossary 22
To Learn More 23
Selected Bibliography 23
Index 24
About the Author 24

ABOUT THE U.S. NAVY SEALs

- The U.S. Navy SEALs were founded in 1962 because the United States needed Special Forces teams with **specialized** training in water.

- SEAL stands for SEa, Air, and Land.

- There are nine SEAL teams. There are about 2,500 SEAL team members.

- SEAL Code:

  » Loyalty to country, team, and teammate

  » Serve with honor and integrity on and off the battlefield

  » Ready to lead, ready to follow, never quit

  » Take responsibility for your actions and the actions of your teammates

  » Excel as warriors through discipline and innovation

  » Train for war, fight to win, defeat our nation's enemies

  » Earn your trident everyday

- SEAL Symbol: trident

SPECIAL TRAINING:

- Antiterrorism: finding **terrorists** and enemies and capturing them

- Intelligence: collecting information through special **reconnaissance missions**

- Rescue: saving people who have been kidnapped by terrorists or other U.S. enemies

Chapter 1

THE ONLY EASY DAY WAS YESTERDAY

It is 6:00 p.m. on Sunday night in Coronado, California. Thirty-nine men scramble on the beach. They are looking for their team members. They also need to find their inflated boats. SEAL trainers shout orders in the darkness. Hell Week has begun.

◀ **Navy SEAL training requires physical and mental strength.**

SEAL training started two weeks ago. It started with 83 men. Only 39 remain. SEAL training is tough. Trainers remind students that, in the real world, SEALs must carry out missions. And they must do so under extreme conditions. Through cold and pain. Even when they can't eat or sleep. SEAL training is meant to be just like war. If a student fails training, he drops out of the program. If a SEAL fails a mission, he or his teammates could die.

With arms linked, students float in the cold ocean water. They must stay there for 15 minutes at a time. Then, in their wet clothes, they work together to carry their boats to the ocean. Then, it's rowing training. One man on the team starts limping. His side of the boat drops. Those around him pick up the extra weight. After all, working together is what the SEALs are all about.

Whistle training exercises are next. The trainer blows his whistle one time. Drop! Two whistles. Crawl! Three whistles. Stand! Then, the teams race across the sand. When they meet the ocean, they are faced with a 4-mile (6-km) swim. The men are wet. Their uniforms are caked with sand. They lift and carry heavy telephone poles. This is building their strength.

▲ **Trainees brace themselves in the cold ocean water.**

Finally, they stop for a few minutes to eat lunch. It's only Monday. But they won't get to sleep until Wednesday. By then, they'll have gone more than 90 hours without sleep. They'll have earned their one-hour sleep break.

At the end of the week, only 19 students remain. They've made it through the first three weeks of SEAL training. The training lasts for six months. On average, seven out of ten students who start SEAL training quit. But at the end of the six months of training, graduates earn the right to wear the **trident** pin. It is the symbol of the SEALs. Those who wear it are part of a brotherhood of warriors.

▲ Trainees run and swim in their full uniforms.

Chapter 2

LEAVE NO MAN BEHIND

It's October 31, 1972. SEAL Team One is helping the South Vietnamese Army fight the North Vietnamese Army. Members are given their mission: sneak onto an enemy naval base to see how it is protected. That night, they slip from their

◀ **A U.S. Navy SEAL Team One member wears camouflage paint on his face during Vietnam operations.**

ship into a rubber boat. The boat's engine roars to life. It slowly makes its way toward land.

It's dark. Landmarks are difficult to see. When the team lands on the beach, they see that the ship's captain has dropped them in the wrong place. But they have a mission to complete. They'll have to set out on foot toward the enemy's base.

For the rest of the night, they sneak around the base. They count weapons and troops. Just before sunrise, they head back to their boat. Before they get to the beach, enemy troops begin shooting at them. The SEALs are outnumbered. They use their radios to call the U.S. Navy ships that are waiting for them. The navy ships will send help. The SEALs know they need to get to the beach, away from the enemy troops.

Before they can get back, one member is shot in the face. Another member refuses to leave his SEAL brother behind. Even if it means he will have to risk his life. With bullets firing all around him, the soldier carries his injured SEAL brother to the beach.

If they can swim out into the sea, they have a chance of being rescued by the navy ships. For the next two hours, the SEAL swims. He holds onto his team member until help arrives. They both survive.

Chapter 3

NEVER GIVE UP

The date is October 3, 1993. Several trucks drive slowly through Mogadishu, the capital of Somalia. The sun burns down on this east African city. Inside the trucks, Special Forces teams, including Navy SEALs, are dressed for battle. Sweat beads down their faces in the heat. Something doesn't feel right, and everyone knows it. SEALs look out the truck's windows, watching for danger.

◀ **Warring in Mogadishu left many parts of the city abandoned.**

Life in Somalia at this time is rough. A war criminal named Mohamed Farrah Aidid is trying to rule Somalia. And he will kill anyone in his way. Today, the SEALs' job is to capture Aidid.

Suddenly, the SEALs hear gunfire. They've driven into a trap. Aidid's men shoot all around them. Thinking quickly, the SEALs steer their trucks out of the city and back to camp. But they hear bad news. Two army helicopters have been shot down. Some of the soldiers on the helicopters survived the crash. But they are surrounded by Aidid's men.

The SEALs know that there is no time for them to rest at base. For the rest of the afternoon, rescue team members move as close to the helicopter crash sites as they can. All through the long night, gun battles rage. U.S. Special Forces try to get around the enemy so that they can rescue the U.S. soldiers. But **ammunition** is running low. The SEALs don't give up. They take turns shooting. This helps save what is left of the ammunition. In the darkness, they move close to the enemy. They are close enough to fight the enemies hand to hand. At the same time, Special Forces teams sneak in and give them more ammunition. By morning, they are able to fight off Aidid's men and save their fellow soldiers.

Chapter 4

FIGHT TO WIN

It's late winter in Afghanistan. Snow piles so high in some places that it reaches the soldiers' waists. A team of 13 Special Forces members treks through the mountain snow. Some drive all-terrain vehicles. The sky is black on this March 2002 evening. As they make their way through the mountains, they must sneak behind enemy lines. The teams split into three groups. Each group needs to find a safe spot and set up a camp. And they need to hurry.

◀ **Armored vehicles are equipped for high-risk missions.**

Early the next morning, U.S. helicopters will be flying through the mountains. The SEALs must make sure that there are no enemy fighters in the mountains. These enemies could shoot the helicopters down.

After hours of traveling, the SEALs find the perfect spot for their camp. But just as they're getting into place, they see that there is a surprise waiting for them. Another camp is there. It is an enemy camp. It is still dark, and the soldiers in the enemy camp are sleeping. The enemy soldiers don't see or hear the SEALs. The SEALs peek over a rocky hill and see a camouflaged tarp. They know that the tarp must be covering something important. The enemy camp is so carefully camouflaged that no one could see it unless they were on the ground and up close. That is why the **satellite** pictures didn't show the camp. From the satellite, the camp looks just like part of the mountain.

The enemy camp has a deadly weapon hiding under the tarp. It is a long-range machine gun. The SEALs know that the gun is strong enough to shoot down helicopters. This is exactly what they have been worried about: a secret enemy camp. The SEALs have to think quickly and move quietly. If they blow their cover, the enemy will attack. The SEALs use their radio to call an army gunship. A gunship is an aircraft that carries heavy weapons. The gunship is nearby. It is waiting to hear from the SEALs. They tell the gunship the location of the camp. Destroy the camp, they tell the gunship.

▲ **Soldiers scan for enemies in the cold mountains of Afghanistan.**

▲ **Soldiers prepare to dig into fighting positions.**

Just in time to protect the U.S. helicopters, the enemy camp is destroyed. The SEALs' training and quick thinking save the U.S. helicopters that fly over the camp a few hours later.

Chapter 5

FAILURE IS NOT AN OPTION

It's late at night on March 20, 2003. Two hundred and fifty SEALs are ready for their next mission. They are on a ship in the Persian Gulf. The sky is dark. The night is hot. One by one, they board smaller boats. The boats move quietly and quickly through the water.

◄ **The Mina Al Bakr was one of the oil platforms the U.S. Navy protected in 2003.**

A few minutes before 10:00 p.m., the boats are in place. The United States is about to **invade** Iraq. But first, the SEALs have to make sure that the oil storage platforms in the ocean are safe. The oil belongs to Iraq. The U.S. government wants to keep the oil safe. But the U.S. government is worried that Iraqis might blow up their own oil to keep it from the United States. The government is worried that the oil might be blown up accidentally during fighting. If that happens, millions of gallons of oil will spill into the water. That would be a disaster for the environment. The SEALs are called in to make a plan to keep the oil safe.

There are five spots where the platforms could be blown up. In order for their mission to be successful, the SEALs have to arrive in all five spots at the exact same time. If they don't, their enemies will guess the SEALs' plan and stop them.

The SEALs check their watches. At exactly 10:00 p.m., their boats speed to the oil terminal. They are dressed for battle, wearing boots and carrying weapons. They have trained for this moment. Silently, they climb up the sides of the platform. Each SEAL arrives at his location on time.

Working quickly, they follow the plan. Move the workers to safety. Find enemy soldiers. Protect the oil. Once again, SEAL

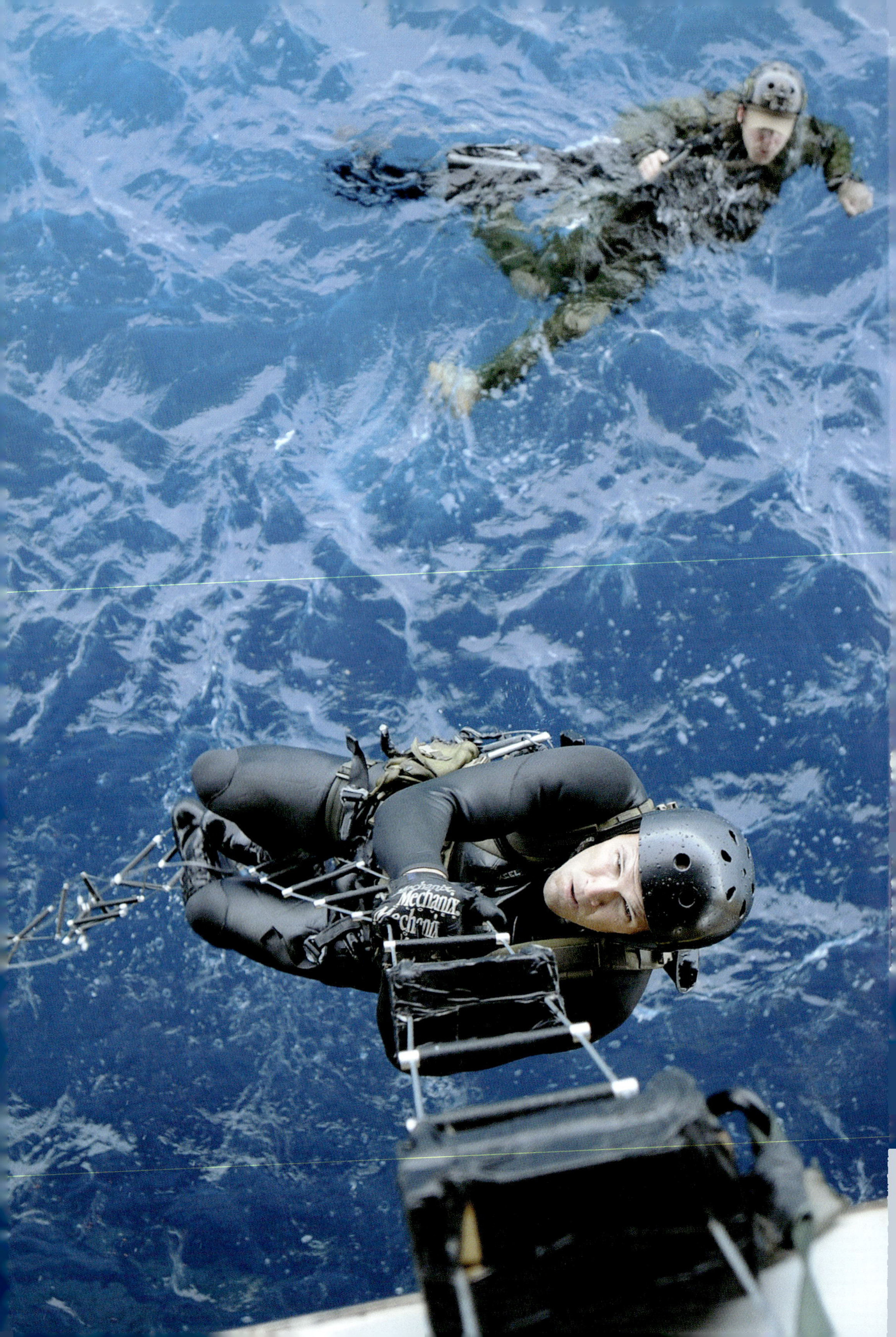
Mechanix

▲ Two soldiers stand watch on the Al Basrah Oil Terminal.

training pays off. By 10:40 p.m., the platforms are safe. U.S. forces have control of them. Enemies cannot get onto the platforms. Army soldiers arrive to guard the platforms. The SEALs head back to their ship after their success. They clean their uniforms and weapons so that they will be ready for the next mission.

◀ SEALs are highly skilled and trained in swimming and water combat.

GLOSSARY

ammunition (am-yuh-NISH-uhn): Ammunition are things such as bullets or shells that can be fired from weapons. The SEALs began to run out of ammunition.

invade (in-VADE): To invade is to enter a country in order to conquer it. The soldiers wanted to invade the small country so that they could take it over.

reconnaissance missions (ree-KAHN-a-suhns MISH-uhns): Reconnaissance missions are missions during which the military observes an area to find an enemy. The Navy SEALs often go on reconnaissance missions to find the enemy.

satellite (SAT-uh-lite): A satellite is a man-made object that orbits the earth. The satellite took pictures of the earth from space.

specialized (SPE-shul-ized): Specialized is to be focused on a specific skill. Navy SEALs are specialized in water training.

terrorists (TER-ur-ists): Terrorists are people who use violence and threats to gain power or force a government to do something. U.S. Navy SEALs are trained to find and capture terrorists.

trident (TRY-dent): A trident is a spear that has three points and looks like a large fork. The Navy SEAL symbol is the trident.

TO LEARN MORE

Books

David, Jack. *Navy SEALs*. Minneapolis: Bellwether Media, 2009.

Whiting, Jim. *Navy SEALs*. Mankato, MN: Creative Education, 2015.

Yomtov, Nel. *Navy SEALs in Action*. New York: Bearport Publishing, 2008.

Web Sites

Visit our Web site for links about missions of the U.S. Navy SEALs: childsworld.com/links

Note to Parents, Teachers, and Librarians: We routinely verify our Web links to make sure they are safe and active sites. So encourage your readers to check them out!

SELECTED BIBLIOGRAPHY

Couch, Dick. *Navy SEALs: Their Untold Story*. New York: William Morrow, 2014.

Durant, Michael J. *In the Company of Heroes*. New York: Signet, 2006.

Naylor, Sean. *Not a Good Day to Die: The Untold Story of Operation Anaconda*. New York: Berkley, 2005.

INDEX

Afghanistan, 14–17
Aidid, Mohamed Farrah, 13
enemy camp, 15, 17
helicopters, 13, 15, 17
Hell Week, 6
invasion, 19
Iraq, 19
machine gun, 15
Mogadishu, Somalia, 12–13
North Vietnamese Army, 10
oil platforms, 19–21
Persian Gulf, 18–19
satellite, 15
SEAL Team One, 10
South Vietnamese Army, 10
Special Forces, 12, 13, 14
training, 6–9, 17, 19, 21
U.S. Navy ships, 11

ABOUT THE AUTHOR

L. S. Haskell has written several books for children, including science, history, biography, and fiction. She lives in Kentucky with her husband and two children.

359.984 H YOU
Haskell, L. S.,
Missions of the U.S. Navy SEALs /

YOUNG
06/16